# The Garden of Magic and Witchcraft

## By Shaya Motamedi

Inspired by Frances Hodgson Burnett's
«The Secret Garden»

Serial Number: P2346250148
Title: The Garden of Magic and Wichcraft
Author: Shaya Motamedi
Illustrator: Mahboobeh
ISBN: 0-037-77892-1-978
Metadata: Junior Fiction, Mystery
Book Size: Paperback
Pages: 100
Canada Publish Date: January 2024
Publisher: Kidsocado Publishing House



KIDSOCADO PUBLISHING HOUSE
Vancouver, Canada

Phone: +1 (833) 633 8654
WhatsApp: +1 (236) 333 7248
Email: info@kidsocado.com
https://kidsocado.com

# For my mom,

This is my first book
which means my first
public dedication!
So, of course it had to be
you. I am beyond glad you
kept pushing me to do this
writing thing.

3> I love you

"All the king's horses and all
the king's men, couldn't put me
together again."

-Taylor Swift

# PROLOGUE

You know that one thing people always say: "the hard days are what make you stronger." Well, I think whatever it is that I'm writing here, captures that sentence perfectly. No- that's a lie.

See how easy it was to fake being happy and strong? I know that people also say "fake it, till you make it," but I've been faking for such an interminably long time that I have seemingly forgotten how to show true, raw emotion.

As you can see, I am not well, so if I seem slightly asinine in some parts, gimme a break.

So, now that the introduction is out of the way, here is my tale, which is perfect for people like you. People who are hurting. Hurting on the inside. People who act like they are fine but have an anger inside them, just waiting to come out. Smiling, beaming in public, but going home to the sound proof walls of their bathrooms, crying; sobbing like they don't already do it everyday.

This story is not here to bring a message and say "everything is going to be okay."

Because it's not.

Well, in my case it wasn't.

You'll see.

# Chapter 1

The air was cold.......

The air was cold. There I was, crouched behind the white SUV, looking up slowly. There they were, my mother, younger sister Sabrina, and my older brother Toby, lying on the side of the road, blood flowing freely everywhere. I wished greatly that I could rush over to them and cry until no more tears came out. But she was still there. Knife in hand, slowly pacing back and forth with a grin on her chalk-pale face. Time seemed to stop. Everything seemed to be quiet.

Until I heard my mother's voice.

"*You need to be careful Maya, you are her. <u>Her.</u> You are.....*"

*She didn't have time to finish her sentence and now she never will.*

*I lay on my belly behind the car, stomach twisting and aching with every breath I took. I was shaking, my heart nearly beating out of my chest, pushing against my rib cage. I wanted to lay here and cry; instead, I pushed down that guilt and fear.*

*I tried to reach for my phone. A shadow moved in the corner of my eye. The sound of a knife falling to the ground pierced through the air. Soon, I was face to face with a creepy figure, her icy blue eyes shining through the darkness.*

*She let out a laugh.*

I woke up with a start, sweat dripping down my face, pooling into my tired eyes.
I have been having that exact dream for the past year and I can't seem to move on.  My body

aches from the lack of peaceful sleep. "This is your life. It has been for the past year, so get up and try to move on, like you *always* do." I told myself confidently.



I practically tripped down the long-marbled staircase for breakfast, passing all the empty rooms. I passed the only room in the house locked with three locks, except two locks were opened and the keys were on the green carpet before it. I was intrigued, but had no choice but to go quickly down for breakfast. Uncle Brian was making French toast and scrambled eggs. My stomach churned at his kindness. I never talk to him, and I feel bad about it. He has never done anything to me, but I don't feel anything enough to have a completely normal interaction with him.

I ate quickly and got ready for school. I should not have to go to school after this whole thing. It's not fair having to lock myself in the girls' washroom everyday just so I could let out my tears. It stings so much to think about it. To think about them. Their pained expressions before their hearts gave out. The way my mother could almost reach out and touch my cheek as I sat with them, sobbing with my head in my bloody hands.

No one could know how it feels being in this state of melancholia.

And it's not like I would tell them.

I cuddled with my dog, Hazel, for a bit before leaving. I took a deep breath as I exited through the door and out into the sunny day.

The grass was green, the sky was blue; the children laughed and ran through the streets, but I couldn't dare to look at them. It brought me memories, sweet memories of my old life.

That only brought me pain.

So, I pushed the thought even further away, until it was shoved far in the back of my mind. For the whole day I did everything as I should and avoided Evie, my old best friend. Because if it wasn't for the fight that she started, I would have gone outside with my family.

Sometimes I like to think that I somehow cheated death because of that, but it doesn't

really help the fact that I am all alone, with the exception of Hazel, my dog, who I am glad survived with me. I avoided everyone. It's not like anyone actually cares if I talk to them. They all seem to either feel sad for me in a sarcastic way, not care, or think that I made it up. Not a lot of people have their whole families get stabbed to death on a road trip.

As soon as I got home, I made myself my beloved NPB sandwich (AKA, Nutella, peanut butter, and bananas), and  went to the door I had seen this morning. I picked up the key and opened the lock. The door opened and there was a pure white glow before me. I stepped in, letting my curiosity get the best of me. Hazel slid in with me. She's a pretty adventurous dog.

The room wasn't really a room it was more like a garden. A *secret garden*. I thought. *Like the book.* Although, I have never seen this garden from the front of the house, even though I could see the road in front of the house. Shocked by what I had come across in this 'room', I felt a small smile escape my lips. The grass was the greenest thing I had ever seen and there were flowers of all colours. When I looked up from the ground, I could again see a bright flash of white in the sky, and just after, everything around me turned a neutral grey, even my clothes. I had on my favourite sweater, a maroon crewneck with dark blue baggy jeans. My short brown hair was down and was also turned grey. Even Hazel was grey. It was honestly sad seeing her in that state of dullness.

In the corner of my eye, I spotted a door covered with vines. The peculiar thing was, I was still grey, all around me was still grey, but that corner where that door lay, was the only colourful thing in the whole garden. I went over to the door and observed it more carefully. There was a single flower that wasn't found in the entire garden, a beautiful periwinkle coloured Lotus with tiny streaks of a vibrant green and blue.

As I curiously opened the wood door, a strong yellow glow overcame the garden and I fell to the ground nauseated.

The last thing I remember was being on the grass, where a creepy girl with blood all over her was looking down at me. I closed my eyes to try to look away.



I couldn't help but scream.

*"Oh, Maya, let's go get some air!"* My mother called out ecstatically. I opened my eyes slowly and stared at the new environment, where, for some very odd reason, I could hear the sweet sound of my mother calling me. It's as if the accident never even happened. As if my own family was not brutally murdered right in front of me. *"Oh my gosh, Maya, just get out of your room we're going for a walk, gosh."* My brother said to me in his old funny voice. He also did his good old hand gesture where he snaps his wrist down. We laughed. My stomach cramped up. Laughing felt so odd now. I felt like even if I were dreaming, I would never feel this much happiness again, from the moment the murder happened. But I went along with whatever that

was happening to me, and I got out of my room and went outside for a walk. The air still smelled salty and the sky was still grey, like in the garden.

I started coughing, but no one came to help me. And suddenly, the idea of their death truly hit me. They were really gone and I was really, truly, alone. Hazel sat down beside me and all I could hear was the silence of my front yard.

# Chapter 2

It was a normal day for the
abandoned...

It was a normal day for the abandoned tower where the deadliest creatures lived, and a semi-normal day for the horrible house right next to the tower, which had humans living in it.

Since the recent arrival of a beautiful girl with glowing eyes and the longest dress, the creatures were in hiding and the large garden around the tower was eerie and dead silent.

In the tower she lived in though, it was chaotic, fumy, and messy. There she was, sitting around the infamous Cauldron of Hell, where many creatures were enchanted, destroyed, and murdered. In her head lived an evil and mysterious plan. A plan that will eliminate those special people in this world.

This girl was a dangerous girl of mystery, Myera, her name coming from the last name *Myers,* simply meaning *evil.*

Police have tried to track her down, but it is impossible, as she is now nearly unstoppable, and the only one that could stop her was still clueless of how powerful they really were.

But this witch, never really thought about this, and she didn't even know how powerful they could be. She just knew, she had to eliminate them, no matter what. Now, all she had to think about was how to do it.

And she started the witchcraft work . . .

# Chapter 3

I opened my eyes slowly.....

I opened my eyes slowly. My surroundings were still grey, but was starting to take shape,and I could see the scene before me much clearer. The trees were moving with the wind as if they were dancing. The birds and squirrels perched in the trees watching. Hazel was also lying down beside me, her fur shedding onto my jeans. I noticed that I wasn't in that part of the garden anymore. In fact, I might not have even been in a garden anymore. I spotted a long tower. It was made of oak and tree bark.

Surrounding it were dozens of cherry blossom trees.

It was a beautiful sight.

There was a shadow of a girl in her teens with two large horns in the ear area. She was hard at work making and testing things with liquid. She suddenly turned her gaze towards me, then whispered: "You are her, and she's coming for you." As she pointed to me, then herself, then held out her bottles of questionable liquid.

Mist started to surround me. Her words rang in my head as I started crawling away from the tower. Three white figures came towards me. "She's coming for you, she's coming for you, she's coming for you." They whispered.

As I started to let out a raw scream, I woke up. Sweat was dripping down my forehead. *Just a bad dream.* I thought. There was still some mist around me.

I was back in my room. I got out of bed and yelled for my uncle. "HELLO?! UNCLE BRIAN WHERE ARE YOU?! Oh hey, Hazel,

come with me." I started to panic. Then, I almost tripped. There, laying on the fluffy white carpet of my room, was the chain for the lock that was on the door of the garden. That chain *never* comes *off* the door, unless something was seriously wrong.

# Chapter 4

I frantically looked around.....

I frantically looked around the massive mansion for my uncle. Hazel just followed me around as I searched. What did the words that the girl said even mean? What if they had been warning me about something? What if I let another family member be in danger?

What if the girl who ruined my life is back? No, that can't be. She's locked up forever.

I thought all these overwhelming thoughts as I

quickly ran around the entire mansion, but Uncle Brian was nowhere in sight. I let out a deep breathe and slowly walked over to the door of the garden. *You're going to be alright; you're going to be fine; you will be JUST FINE*, I told myself.

I started to sob violently again. I couldn't breath. I was shaking. I clung to my chest. No, this can't be happening right now. Not right now. Before it could get any worse, I stepped into the beam of light in the door. I felt a tug as I softly landed on the grass of the garden. There was a shy little girl with pigtails and small light denim overalls. She was holding a purple and pink teddy bear with a red heart in its chest.

I must have looked like I was a tomato drowning in tears because she looked at me with much sadness and concern. Her sad blue-grey eyes sparkled against the grey of the sky. I couldn't help but feel warm around her. She mentioned for me to follow her. She brought me to a part of the garden that had another oak door with a single rare lotus flower and vines. On the left was a pond with swans and ducks swimming around. She put her teddy bear on the ground

and looked at me, eyes beaming. "I'm Maddie, and welcome to the garden, what's your name? How did you end up here?" The little girl said, first quietly, then more enthusiastically. "Hi, I'm Maya, this is my dog, Hazel." I said just as Maddie pet Hazel softly. "So, um . . ." I continued. "The house next door is my uncle's and . . . ." I paused. Was it worth telling her about the past year? "Well, about a year ago, my family and I went on a road trip to Oregon, and then they were killed." I said. I had to leave out the part where I woke up screaming in the middle of the night. Every night. Or crying during the day. "Aw, I'm sorry, but seriously, you live THERE?" She asked, pointing to Uncle Brian's house. "That's the house everybody in this garden fears." Then she started to whisper: "Even Myera fears him and the power the house has."

"Who's Myera?" I asked. "Myera, is the feared child of Medusa (although she isn't very similar), she has been here for the past year and has been making trouble ever since! She has been destroying and enchanting everything and spends hours in the wooden tower in the heart of the garden. Nobody knows what she is working towards, but we know its going to be bad, and the crazy part is, around 6 months ago, the animals have disappeared and Myera has been working harder and harder, and yet, no one knows why." Maddie spoke in a way so poetic I found myself captivated in listening to her words. As if they were a poem. Even Hazel seemed interested.

As all of this was being processed in my head, I realize that this is real. My dream could have been warning me about this Myera girl, witch, or whatever she was. And the tower too, it was shown in my weirdly clear and specific dream. "How do you know all this?" I asked Maddie when she stopped circling playfully around me. She looked at me sadly. "My mom disappeared two years ago and I will never forget the day she told me her biggest secret. She had a garden in her childhood house where she grew up. When she took me there, she showed me the garden and a wooden door with a single rare flower that was only found in that area. She explained how the flower was the key to success, beauty, and enchantment. If found in the wrong

hands, the flower could be used as a spell, and depending on how powerful the person is, could potentially end the world forever. Only a tiny percentage



of the world, known as *idiosyncratic people*, have the power to stop it, but every time the flower was used to curse someone, that population was too late, or hadn't discovered their powers yet. And only about one tenth of that percentage found out their powers. She also let me into the oak door and we stepped in, but she disappeared into the light, and I never saw her again. Let me be honest with you, I am one of the people with the secret hidden powers. My mom was also one of them. And I know she would want me to be helping anyone who stumbles upon our secret." Maddie said. I stared at her in amazement. "So, have you been here since you and your mom went through the door?" I asked her. "Yes." She answered sadly.

I wondered if she would ever find her again. Maybe at least she would get her mom back. "I know what you're thinking, and yes, my power is mind reading, but I've looked everywhere that I can, I haven't found her yet." "Everywhere you can? Does that mean there are places you can't go?" I asked curiously. Maddie sighed helplessly. "You have way too many questions girl." She said with a laugh. I grew anxious. I hate making people feel annoyed. "There is a part of the garden where Myera is, she has an oak tower where she works day and night, and she has protected it with some sort of thing, so if my mom, and maybe your uncle are there, we won't be able to get to them." She continued. "But the powers that people got were able to stop any witchcraft, so that means, if we round up and find most of the special people, and use the powers together, we could stop Myera!" I said. I felt my brain finally working after such a long time. Maybe doing whatever this was would distract me from everything. An escape plan. One adventure to save myself. I started towards the oak door to get out of the garden so that we could start with this plan. But as I tried to pull the door open, the door wouldn't budge even an inch! "Uh, but slight problem." I said. "The door won't open."

# Chapter 5

I was pacing back and forth,.....

I was pacing back and forth, trying to figure out what to do here. Maddie was looking up at the sky, whispering words I could not hear. Hazel just spun around, matching my energy.

"Wait, Maddie! Is there any way that you could tell what Myera is thinking right now? It could help us- somehow." I said quickly without thinking of what might happen. "Yes, I will, but first, I think I can somehow project it onto something so that we can both hear it." Maddie answered. She held her pointer finger to each side of her head. After about two minutes, Maddie had created a clear image in the pond, and what it was showing was so bad, it could hurt so many people and nobody would even notice! Myera had a plan so evil, it was hard to imagine. The pond showed a girl with short, wavy brown hair with horns on her head mixing potions and liquids. She had glowing purple and red eyes as she stared at her evil potions. She looked oddly familiar. Her plan was to hypnotize the people and bring them to her, where she will then eliminate all their powers. The image in the pond showed Myera stabbing a teenage boy's wrist as he sat there, wailing, blood gushing out of him. He just lay there, dying.

We both gasped at the horrifying image. She took the powers out of his blood and stored it in a jar filled halfway with other people's powers, just waiting to be made into something that could be very disastrous. I didn't dare think about what would happen if the jar completely filled up. As for the blood, to me and Maddie's surprise, Myera drank the blood straight from the cup she had poured it into, and as she swal-

lowed the blood, her eyes stopped glowing and her whole face grew soft, her eyes turning to the colour of salt water. For a split second, she seemed to hesitate on her plans.

She looked like someone I never thought I would see again.

"Mom?" I cried just as she looked at me and the image in the pond cleared.

Before I knew it, I was kneeling on the perfectly green grass, feeling the tears running down my cheeks. Hazel rushed over to me and I cried into her fur. Maddie knelt beside me, rubbing my shoulder to comfort me. She said to me, "I have to tell you something. I lied to you in the beginning. My mom didn't disappear into the light she.... my mother was caught doing witchcraft deep in this garden and was turned into an enchanted animal. She roamed the gardens for about two years before she was shot by ... It's hard to say this, but she was shot by your uncle. A little part of me said that she deserved it because witchcraft is the most appalling form of magic there is, but the rest of me cried and cried, and I felt like I would never feel like my true being until finding out about my powers. That was when I felt good being able to always know what is on someone's mind. And as my mom always said, "As long as there is love and memory, there is no true loss." Maddie's words were so poetical I started calming down knowing there was someone that understood me even though our situations were different.

I stood up, clearing my throat; wiped my tears and quickly said, "I think we're running out of time, anybody else in the magical community could be next in Myera's evil plan, so I think we should recruit the 'magical' people in this area and round up as much of them as we can and try to save the hostages of Myera waiting to be killed by this elimination process, so we have to move quick." I finished. "But the oak door is somehow locked, so how do we get out?" Maddie questioned.

I went to the door and pulled (and pushed) as hard as I could and fell on my bum. I prayed greatly that I could actually do something. It has been so long since I actually got up on my butt and did anything at all. Don't get me

wrong, I do my homework, but that only helps me get closer to getting a worthless piece of paper at the end of high school. Even if it creates the smallest dent, I want to take the credit, I want to know always and forever that I did something. Something amazing. Something that leaves a mark. Something good. And I want to always remember that it was me. Me, who did it. It is kind of selfish I know. I put my head against the door and felt the design of the oak with my fingers and made lines as I closed my eyes. I concentrated and murmured, "Ever tried. Ever failed. No matter. Try again. Fail better." I smiled. "Did your mom ever say that to you?" Maddie said. I knew I couldn't say no because it was true, and she could literally read my mind. "Yeah, it truly gives me hope." I answered. I waited for her to say something else, but she was looking straight behind me. I turned around and to my surprise, there it was, the oak door swung open.

# Chapter 6

"How did you do that?"

"How did you do that?" Maddie asked in awe. I shrugged. Me and Maddie slowly walked towards the oak door and stepped outside the garden for the first time since what felt like hours of talking and explaining. *What if, I was part of the population and I had... powers?* The thought sounded so ridiculous and childish. Like something out of a book about *rainbows* and *fairies* and *magic.* But there was no other logical explanation to how I opened the door. "Could someone else be behind the door opening by itself?"

Maddie said, reading my thoughts. I knew that she was reading my mind and searching deeper for how that happened. "Maya, you opened the door, and the only way to find out if you are part of the magical community is . . ." She paused. Then, out of nowhere a piece of shimmering purple cloth was wrapped around me. "What is happening?" I asked. "This is the Cloth of Magic and if after the cloth is removed from your body, it starts flying, it means you areand magical, and if its falls to the ground, you are just a normal being." Maddie answered me. After a minute, the cloth was removed, and to my surprise, it didn't fly nor fall. Instead, it floated and glowed a very light yellow. "Interesting." Maddie said. "This reaction is very rare." "Well, what does it mean?" I asked, puzzled. "I'm not really sure, but it does signify that you are a magical being and you are more powerful than the rest of the normal population. But it also means you can control both witchcraft and magic itself. In most cases, the being can choose to be part of either the good or evil, since they're able to control both types.

But again, it's very rare." Maddie spoke in a very scientific way, as if I was a very interesting science project. I gasped at her knowledge and at this weird discovery about myself.



I sighed. I didn't want to be a special being. I didn't intend on actually being something special. I stared at my hands while they were trembling. Maddie rubbed my back in a way that made me feel warm.

Never, in my almost fourteen years of life, had I imagined this scene right here, and weirdly, I was grateful for it.

I made a good friend and a couple memories while it lasted.

And as much as everything hurts, she helped me open up empathetically in ways I could never have imagined.

# Chapter 7

So, for the next hour or.....

So, for the next hour or so, I was either thinking of what to even start with, or, I was just sulking. Suddenly, I heard a faint and quiet whisper coming close. And closer . . .  Then, out of the blue, came a ghostly girl. She seemed lonely and frightened. Though, as she got closer, I noticed that she was growing older, taller, even. Soon, she turned into a beautiful girl with luscious brown hair and bright blue eyes. She almost looked like . . . "MOM!" Maddie yelled. Her mother started to reach out to her. They seemed to go into a hug. She even hugged me, but soon I realized that something was itching at me. Her hug was so familiar, the way she laughed, the way her hands felt smooth like hand cream. As Maddie's mother morphed into my mother, I felt like I *needed* to breath, but I just couldn't. It felt as though my *soul* was getting stolen. It sounds stupid I know, but trust me, I *couldn't breath.* My fight or flight was getting tested. I guess I chose somewhat of a version of *fight.* I quickly snatched the flower on the oak door and shielded my face as if it was going to shield me from a gun. My mother stopped whatever she was doing quickly. She stared hard at the flower, and just as suddenly as she came, she faded away into flower petals. Maddie seemed impressed, but the look on her face showed interest like there was something else she wasn't telling me. *Damn it! I wish I could read her mind like she can with mine.* I thought angrily. Suddenly a voice that sounded like Maddie ringed in my head.

**"Why was she fighting her mom with her anger?"**

"She was so smart to think of the rare flower trick."

"It's so weird how she's capable of both magic and witchcraft which is neither good nor bad."



"Her mother must have been capable of magic, but also witchcraft, explaining how she could have been Myera."

"But why? And I thought she died along with the rest of Maya's family. Gosh I feel so bad for her."

Why did she think all that? If I don't commit neither magic nor witchcraft, what does that make me? Am I an outcast again, even out of the *idiosyncratic* people? Am I just some *creature*? Anger boiled inside me. I started feeling like I *couldn't trust Maddie.* But I had to.

For now.

Slowly I felt this odd anger just jumping out. I felt a very strong light on my eyes. Then, everything became very black. Perhaps,the blackest of blacks, a flat black.

I was neither floating nor walking. I was just

casually bouncing up and down the area. Out of nowhere, a creepy figure appeared. It was in the shape of me and moved as I moved.

Just my own shadow.

I kept bouncing down what seemed to be a flat hallway that never seemed to end. I kept going anyways, until my shadow somehow stayed in front of me, not moving as I moved. It stopped me and I froze. The shadow started to grow tall. Then it started to shrink, and I watched in horror as the shadow turned out to be Myera. Her appearance was much different than how she looked before. She was much chubbier and had lots of warts on her misshaped face. Her hair was not brown anymore but an ugly black-green. *"Those are the effects of witchcraft."* I heard Maddie's poetic voice ring in my head.
She walked slowly towards me, and to my surprise, slapped me across the face, which unfortunately triggered a few terrifying memories.

I felt the burn on my cheek. Clutching my face, I looked around and in front of me was a middle-aged woman with brown hair, chubby

cheeks, eyeliner, and bright red lipstick, along with layer after layer of shiny lip gloss. "MAYA WILLOW ORTEGA! ARE YOU EVEN LISTENING TO ME?!"



It was the sound of my angry mother. I missed my mom a lot, but now, I remember all the memories of her saying I wasn't perfect, and how I was the worst daughter in the world when I got in trouble. But beyond that, I will always remember her sweet smile, her soft healing hands, her amusing laughter. "MAYA! Ugh, you never listen to me, you flawed young lady!" My mom stormed into another room. As soon as she left, my little sister walked into the room with a fearful look. She had been listening to the conversation the whole time. "Maya, is Mommy going to leave us? Like Daddy did?" Sabrina asked me with so much sadness in her eyes.

All was silent.

"No, of course not Sabrina." I said with so much pain in my voice.

Tears formed in my eyes as I thought about

how much anger and sorrow I have stored in my chest since I was 8 because of a stupid man who took his family for granted. I wiped the tears away and hugged Sabrina tightly. Suddenly all the light seemed to disappear and now, everything was dark.

I was back in the dark hallway.

Sabrina started to grow older and taller too, then pulled me closer by the sleeve of my sweater. "How could you leave us outside the car when we were being freaking murdered!" My stomach cramped with guilt. "I was really upset that day from my fight with Evie, I didn't want to get out of the car, I didn't know that it was going to happen!" I said while blinking back tears.

"You are no sister of mine." Sabrina said coldly.

*I am losing my love for you,* her disdainful voice summarized. Before I could say anything else, a voice called, "SABRINA, COME HERE THIS INSTANT!" "Yes, mother." Was all that Sabrina replied and quickly dashed away. I

looked in Sabrina's direction, then turned back to where I had been looking at. I saw myself looking straight into my older brother Toby's face. He looked depressed and sad, but serious. I quickly looked away before I made any eye contact with him. I looked down and saw Hazel lying beside Toby's legs. Why is Hazel here? I thought as I bent down and scratched him behind the ears and pet his soft light brown fur. Tears started streaming down my face when I came to realization that my family was in heaven and I would actually never see them again.

As I was petting Hazel, Toby stood there, listening to the silence of the hallway. He suddenly made eye contact with me. "She wants to see you." He whispered. I looked at him confused. "Who?" I whispered back. "Who else? *Mother*." Toby replied coldly. We walked through the darkness until we finally reached an oak door. It looked strangely like the two oak doors in the garden. It also had the exact same rare flower held up by different coloured vines.
*I wonder if Maddie is wondering where I am*

*or if I'm okay? Does she even care that much?* I thought with a new, burning feeling in my chest. "Have fun." Toby said in a very off version of his funny sarcastic voice. I realized how much I miss him. He was never even close to being the best sibling, but we had good times. Good laughs.

Its time to move on, I told myself. After all, this is all a dream that will be gone in just a minute, with everyone included; I could finally get back to my plan.

The door suddenly swung open and there she was, inside the infamous oak tower, my mother. Keeping watch of everything outside it. I saw myself in the mirror.

*I look just like her.*

For a moment, I forgot everything about the fact that my mom was, or is Myera. That she is using magic (and witchcraft) for evil, or that she is in possession of a very rare flower. I just completely forgot. All I thought about was the murder of my mother and how much I missed and longed for her from the moment she lay

bloody on the ground. All the flashbacks of the terrible evening that ruined my life. Her on the ground. Blood everywhere. Blood. Fear. Her worried expression, whatever it was, it never left her face. The face I so loved and always will. The now old face of my own mother who was always there for me. Tears rolled down my cheeks when I ran to hug her tightly. But just as I touched her, she and all my surroundings, the room, the dark hallway, disappeared and faded into the light.

Page:

61

# Chapter 8

The light led me back .....

The light led me back to the garden where both Maddie and Hazel rushed over to me. "Okay, what the hell just happened?" Maddie asked, deeply concerned about me. Through my loud sobs I explained everything. From the flat dark hallway, to seeing Toby and Sabrina, and how I saw my mother. Maddie was really interested to know. After I was done, she said, "Well, while you were gone, I thought of something. Something big. So, you know how you thought about what would happen if Myera completely filled up her jar of power?"

I nodded. "Well, depending on what the power *really is*, I think that if the jar is full, there is literally nothing we can do. Myera is able to steal any magical being's heart and/or soul, using the potion." She stopped to get my re-action. I was listening but was also zoned out. Does she mean that, what happened with that ghost earlier . . . was a sign? Obviously, Maddie heard it and she suddenly went quiet. "I think, maybe you're right, it was a sign, a message. Just like those dreams you had, Maya. Myera has been calling you and giving you signs and clues since your family was . . . assassinated. She was calling you.

*"She still is"*

*She was calling me all along?* I slowly thought to myself. Why is this happening to me? All I want is to go to my bed and sleep for hours until the light of the next morning comes and I could wake up and see the face of Sabrina in our room. Our old room. "So, step 1, figure out how to recruit those people. Step 2, find my mom, and your uncle. Step 3, Find Myera, and step 4, save the idiosyncratic people from Myera."

Maddie said only just thinking of the plan on the spot. "Step 4  seems like *a lot* of steps." I said. "But let's go anyways." I continued. Because we really are just winging it. And off we went. Out of the garden, out of the mansion, and onto the dark, empty streets.

An unlikely group. A thirteen-year-old, a nine-year-old and a golden retriever.

# Chapter 9

We stood there for at least .....

We stood there for at least 15 minutes after we left the house. "How do we even start?" I said with impatience. "I guess we travel the world?" Maddie said with uncertainty. "No, there has to be a better way." I muttered to myself.

And then the whole world turned green. A dark, luscious green.

I opened my eyes to find tree branches in my face. Maddie and Hazel appeared behind me. We were all very confused. What had just happened? We were in what seemed to be another garden just like ours, but instead of an oak door, there was a door made of red cedar tree bark, but the flower on the door and everything else was the same. I looked to my left and there it was, a giant house sitting right next to the garden. This made everything crystal clear to me. "No way!" Maddie said smiling. *Yes way!* I thought. I had brought us to one of the idiosyncratic people's homes with their own secret garden.

"Wait, so this means that the population that we call idiosyncratic, they all have a secret garden in their home? Does the person who built the houses know that the next owner is going to be one of them?" I ask. "No, I don't think so, I think that the secret garden is just a message, a sign that you are one of them, and it just moves in with you at every house." Maddie answered quickly. "Also, Maya, I mean obviously you are special like all of us, but even your power is special. You can both wish for something and even what you *think of* can come true . . . oh wait, let's hope that you haven't thought any bad things,

but just, you know, be careful."

*Be careful.*

A phrase that has been said to me way too many times throughout my life, and now, it just doesn't seem so possible anymore.

# Chapter 10

### We stayed there a while .....

We stayed there a while just staring at one of our fellow... idiosyncratic people's secret garden. They probably didn't even know that it was there. It took at least five minutes until I slowly walked towards their own garden's oak door. Maddie trailed behind. I opened the door, fearing what happened last time to happen again. When the light blinded me.

It did. But something unexpected happened.

I was floating somewhere, sort of downwards, with Hazel in my arms. It was as if I were falling, but very slowly. Maddie was there beside me this time.

There was a faint green glow below us, the part we were going towards. We suddenly landed with a thud. We were in another world of grass. Maddie stood up but as quickly as she did, she dropped to the ground again. I suddenly felt something tingly. My nose was filled with many exhausting scents, and I soon became weary and lay in the grass.

The last thing I remember seeing was a girl with blood smeared all over, standing above me, looking straight into my eyes, her icy blue eyes staring creepily right into my soul, before the whole world went black.

Again.

# Chapter II

## Something like this had .....

Something like this had happened to me before.

When I was 8 years old.

It was the day after my father left. I shouldn't have cried the way I did that morning. Because he was never my *dad*, he was just my *father*.

But I cried. I cried so much I got dizzy and the world went dark. For hours. I would open my eyes now and then but the darkness was comforting. It distracted me from the pain.

I was in my bed for so long everyone was worried.

But no one was thinking about my mother. Because she was the one who cared for him. All the years that they were married.

And he just left her like that.

After probably 3 whole days, I stirred out of bed.

I will never forget the anger on my mom's face.

I woke up, dizzy.

The world was blurry but it's starting to come into shape now.

Everywhere was misty.

My breathing was shaky.

The malodorous smell of the flowers exhausted me to an awful point.

Maddie woke up, half unconscious beside me.

I felt like I was trapped in a closet full of plants.

I tried to sit up but quickly fell back onto the grass, my eyes heavy, the world becoming dark again as I felt my heavy eyes close, fearing I may not open them again.

Page:

83

# Chapter 12

The world was hazy .....

*The world was hazy and misty.*
*I still lay unconscious on the grass. But I could make*
*out some figures again.*

*A tall figure stood above me.* "Don't forget.
Everyone will turn their back on you eventually. Even
yourself. You are her Maya._ Her._ You know it.
Don't even try to deny it."

I woke up feeling a sense of misunderstanding
and heartbreak in my chest.

*How long had I been unconscious? Is Maddie okay?*
*Is she even here-?*

Suddenly, everything went dark for maybe a fraction of a second, before a tall lady appeared before me. I stood up, ready to run. "Hey, its you!" She called out in a deep, alluring voice.

I was bewildered. It's me? What does that even mean? My eyebrows shot up to my hairline once I realized. "So, you are . . . me - from the future?" I asked. "Oh, don't sound so foolish and childish young lady, of course, yes, it is you that is me standing here. You see, this whole situation, from the moment you family was murdered, sparked, how do I put this in words that you'll understand? Basically it formed a *crack* in the universe. Because, well, the universe was aware of the fact that something that reveals your whole entire future was put in your head. All the dreams and "visions" you've had the past, well exactly 368 days plus the days you've been in this whole new, strange world, were signs. You following? Okay great, I'm going to continue either way. And, here I am *continuing* to reveal your future because you would have either way found out when you would have come to stop me."

"Wait, you're Myera-" I reply. Suddenly, everything made sense. My mother's last words, my most recent vision. And I also realized that the Myera I saw in my visions were all me. Not my mother. *I am evil.* I turn out as an evil girl.

Something seemed to twist in me. Like it was being put into place. I realized that the always livid grey sky turned a deep blue. The wound in the universe was being restored. But the wound inside me is not. It never will be.

I realize what my future must be. I'm, as it turns out, a murderer. A killer.

# Epilogue

So, there you have it, the most useless survivor story ever told. And yet, if you're reading this, that means that this was in some way intriguing for you. And that's great, really. I adore getting the recognition that I deserve, but, really think about it, what does liking the pain of this tale say about you, huh? Do you enjoy reading about the tragedies that go on in my head? That pain inside me, as agonizing as it is, I have to live with it. And I do live with it now.

This is just my life. At least, maybe I am still the greatest woman out there. At least, I did do something. Maybe, I finally am the best at something. At least sooner rather than later, the wound in me will heal.

I'm glad to even be delusional about it because deep down I know that the wound inside me will never heal. It will always be there, burning and churning in my heart, haunting me with my past.

Sometimes the pain got so unbearable that I would daydream about my childhood. The days of running in fields, sunshine beaming on my face, path wide and open. I would just run and run, not knowing anything about the world, as I had not learned about the world yet, and

the world had yet to hurt me.

Those memories were freedom as I knew it.



Until I would get to the memories of when my life went downhill.

That stupid, stupid day.

Sadly when I started to dream, I couldn't stop. I remembered this dream vividly. I was hiding behind the car door, wind pushing at my face. It would start to rain soon, I would think, as I got up to grab my phone that was thrown across the pavement. I reached and reached, fingertips almost touching the edge of the screen, so close to grabbing and calling someone, anyone. And then I would hear the sharp ping of the knife slicing the air, dropping onto the ground. The ground in front of me. Inches away from my face.

I would slowly stand up, hoping the slower it took, the faster she would go away.

But she didn't. She stayed. In my head. And she would always stay. For the rest of my existence. I can't really call it life at this point, when I am only thinking of past memories, again and again.

I do realize that I am rambling again, but I can't help myself any more than I couldn't help them. Mom, Sabrina, and Toby. On that stupid, stupid day.

Had they been a dream? I ask myself with deep concern, because why couldn't I remember them?

Yet I could still hear her laugh. That deadly, horrifying laughter. Icy and cold, like the eyes that I couldn't stop looking at when we came face to face.

I don't know why I am like this. What the purpose is. Why it feels like an endless dream.

Endless yet painful. Oh, so painful. It burns.

And it won't stop. I don't know what I am supposed to do.

I don't know when I'm going to wake up again.

I woke up with a start, sweat dripping down my face, pooling into my tired eyes.

I felt confused because I was sure I'd had this dream before.

THE END

# Aknowledgments

The biggest thanks I have to give right now is to Kidsocado for having an advertisment at a fashion event where they helped me finally achieve my dream (since I was 9) of publishing a book! I also greatly thank Ms. King who was my grade 5 teacher, I love writing and she really made me feel like I was good at what I like to do. So, thank you for making us write creepy stories (even though this didn't turn out to be the spooky version) on October 30th, 2020.

Because I would've never written this book.

## Author Biography

Shaya Motamedi is an Iranian- Canadian grade 8 student, who has had a love for writing since she was in the third grade. She enjoys reading horror & thriller novels. Her other passions include being on her school's basketball team and playing the piano.

Shaya currently lives with her family in Vancouver, British Columbia located in southwest of Canada.

The Garden of Magic and Witchcraft is her first published book, initially written when she was eleven years old.